In A Relationship with Success

Flairs and Glairs
Publication House

"In a Relationship with Success"

ISBN No: " 978-93-90799-64-0"
1st Edition
Language – English and Hindi

Flairs and Glairs
Publication House
Regd. Under MSME Act.

Disclaimer

This is a work of fiction and solely represent the thoughts of the corresponding authors of the articles. Our editors have tried their best to edit the content of all the authors and check the plagiarism.
All the write-ups in this book are unique and are only published in this book.
In case any plagiarism or error is found, only the author is responsible alone, and not the publisher or the Compilers.

Cover Designing and Book Formatting
Shubham Shah and Ishani Agarwal

Acknowledgement

Hi all,
We would like to acknowledge the following as being idealistic channels and fresh dimensions in the completion of this anthology.
We take this opportunity to thank God, our parents and acknowledge their contribution of whatever we are today is just because of them.
I would like to thank the publication for providing the necessary facilities required for completion of this anthology.
Thank you to each and every co-author for being a part of this book and for submitting their beautiful write-ups to make this book more special.
Big thanks to all those who have in any way contributed to this anthology.

Thank you!
Now, let's catch up to "In A Relationship With Success".

<u>Co-authors</u>

Shubham Shah (Founder Flairs and Glairs)
Ishani Agarwal (Co-Founder Flairs and Glairs)
Pragya Verma (Compiler)

1. Tuhina Sharma
2. Ankeeta Sahani
3. Padma Srivastava
4. Adya Kumar
5. Yachika Prajapati
6. Christy Gnana Deepa J.
7. Rohan
8. Abshaar Ibrahim
9. Arya Ojha
10. Vishali S.
11. Aasifa Khanam
12. Sakshi Jain
13. Ankita Mahana
14. Shivani M. R. Joshi
15. Sanjay Naik
16. Isha Vaghela
17. Arundhati Shekar
18. Deepshikha Nathawat
19. Gunjan Jogia
20. Sirisha Susarla
21. Sahina Ghugha
22. Ankita Bhatia
23. Joydeep Mallik
24. Sanoj Kumar
25. Sakshi Jain
26. Jeevitha. S
27. Vaishnawi Kumari
28. Sushmita Mishra
29. Nivetha R C

30. Kareena Verma
31. Gaurav Sharma
32. Krishna Motwani
33. Nafisha Mullick
34. Shubhashish Ranjan
35. Keerthana Suriya
36. Aman Siddiqui
37. Darshan Patel
38. Harshita Verma
39. Ayushman Majhi
40. Muskan Sachdeva
41. Debesh Prusty
42. Sabbi Ansari
43. Kavita Bhatt
44. Sharvari Sangam Patil
45. Pratham Mittal
46. Jayashree Sahoo
47. Ipsita Panigrahi
48. Archishman Satpathy
49. Aman Sharma
50. Vivek Santosh

Shubham Shah

(Founder- Flairs and Glairs)

Shubham Shah, an entrepreneur at "Flairs & Glairs" a brand with dynamics in events organizing and cultural educational pan INDIA, is a 26yrs old guy who recently has entered the digital platform of imprinting emotions. He has initiated with his own open mic platform to help budding poets and aspiring writers under his brand named as "Teekhe Zasbaaat"

He is a commerce graduate from the Bhagalpur City of Bihar. He states Writing has impersonated him since childhood and he has now been writing for over a decade!
Cooking, on the other hand, is his passion! He also mentions, trying out new things just tickles him!
When asked sir, Why SPICY EMOTIONS?
He smiled and added, "agar jasbaat teekhe na ho toh wo jasbaat kahan" Spices are all that blends! So do his words!
As a chef, he presents to you his dish! Hot and freshly served! Taste it! Feel it! Enjoy it! You can also find his writing in the Book "Teekhe Zasbaaat" and 50+ Co-authored anthologies. With his passion to explore opportunities across Platforms, he is working with keen devotion and We wish him all the very best for his future ventures.
He is Featured in the **International Magazine De-Mode** for his upcoming solo novel.
He is **Approved by Ne8x for its Lit Fest,** and is a **Golden Star Awards 2020 Winner.**
He is an **India Book of Records Holder** for his Anthology **Satrang,** and has the **Grandmaster** title by **Asia Book of Records**, for the same.
He has also been featured in **Prabhat Khabar**, **Dainik Jagran** and other renowned Newspaper for his achievements.
He has also been awarded with **India Star Republic Award 2021.**
He has been a proud co-author to
India Book of Records (Title- Black)
World Book of Records (Title -15 Wonders of Poetries)
India Book of Records (Title - Aaina)
Vajra World Records Holder (Title - Gustakhi Maaf Hai)
High Range of Records Holder (Title - Gustakhi Maaf Hai)

Share your reviews on his

INSTAGRAM

@spicy_emotions
@shubham4shah

Or via email on

shubham2shah@gmail.com

To stay tuned to his work and opportunities follow his business Handles

INSTAGRAM FACEBOOK YOUTUBE

@flairsandglairs
@teekhezasbaaat

WEBSITE:

https://flairsandglairs.in/
https://flairsandglairs.com/

Ishani Agarwal

(Co-Founder- Flairs and Glairs)

Ishani Agarwal hails from the City of Joy, Kolkata.
She is the co-founder of her Community "Teekhe Zasbaaat" and Flairs and Glairs Publication.
Been a Compiler for 45+ Anthologies, she is in the process for more. Co-authored in 150+ Anthologies. She is a India Book of Records Holder, a Vajra World Records Holder, a High Range of Records Holder and a Bravo Record holder.

Approved by Ne8x for its Lit Fest 2020, and Literary Icon 2020. Also a Golden Star Awards Winner 2020.
She has also been awarded with India Star Republic Award 2021.
She has been featured by the National Magazine "Taree Zameen Par" with the title 'unstoppable'.
Also featured in the International Magazine DeMode for her upcoming solo novel, she is proud to write on social issues, and is happy with the love she is receiving.
Connect with her on Instagram: @Ishani_agarwal_quotes / @compilations_so_far

Pragya Verma

(Compiler)

Pragya Verma was born on 21 March 2001 in Prayagraj, Uttar Pradesh. She is currently pursuing Bachelor of Computer Applications from Ewing Christian College, Prayagraj. She has studied from Jagat Taran Golden Jubilee School.

This is her second book which she has compiled with lots of hard work and immense love. This book is her baby and it will always remain close to her heart. She has also compiled anthology named as, "Shades of Night".

She is a poetess and a writer. She loves to write English poetry and articles and she also writes Hindi poems, shayari, microtales and quotes. She has done 107+ anthologies, she has been a part of three world record anthologies and four international anthologies as a co-author. She has got 41 publishing certificates as a co-author of many anthologies.

She has a great interest in making paintings and doing photography. She has won many writing competitions and has

got 23 achievement certificates, 17 appreciation certificates and 32 participation certificates.
She has also taught many children as a tuition teacher as she loves to teach children. She loves to gain spiritual knowledge and tries to find peace everywhere. She is a wanderlust person. She wanted to see and explore every corner of this world. She just loves to explore new places, take photos and keep it all as a memory.
She has started writing from 2019 and in September 2020, she started doing anthologies that gave her a platform to show her writing talent.
Now, she is a Published Author.

You can contact her through-
Email: pragyaallahabad34@gmail.com

Instagram Handle: @wordsofpragya ,
@pragyaxart , @pragya.vermaa

Stay Headstrong

Here, survival is hard,
Struggles that you can't discard.
Have loneliness in your heart?
Just make it your weapon and restart.

When depression calls, don't pick it up,
Let your soul relax and don't give up.
Finding peace can be hardest,
All you have to do is to shine in your darkest.

Sometimes your mind will form unstoppable storms,
Sometimes it will fill you with painful thorns.
Don't let it hurt you in any way,
Keep control on your mind and make it a better place to stay.

Stay headstrong in every situation,
In your life, you are the only one who can bring illumination.

Break All Obstacles

"Don't remove obstacles, just break them,
You are the real warrior, show them."

Clear your mind, give it positive thoughts and positive vibes. That's the first step of getting success.

Shift yourself away from all distractions. Pull them out from roots and throw them away.

If you have courage then fine if not, then create courage to leave everything that's very close to your heart but still distracting you from achieving your goals.

Don't give up on your dreams, give up on your sleep, give up on the things that won't help you in winning.

Love yourself as much as you can as self-love is necessary to achieve anything. If you will love yourself then only you will love to fulfill your own dreams and that dream will give you determination to achieve your goal and get success.

Sometimes life becomes heavy and at that time you don't want to do anything. At that time, let yourself burst out, cry or shout or do whatever you want to do but just do something to release out this heaviness.

And after that, tell yourself that you are with yourself. You're not going to leave yourself in any situation or any phase of life. You have to tell yourself that you have to stay strong in this situation to get back and start working on your dreams and to get what you always wished to get.

Plan in your own mind or write it down that what are the tasks you have to complete today or tomorrow. The work that is most important do that immediately and do your all work day by day according to the importance of the work.

Don't lose hope. Complete your own work on time, don't wait for anybody else's work to get completed and then you'll do your own. Don't postpone your work thinking that you'll do it when the last day will come.

Write your progress. Smile and become happy after seeing that you've done what you've never thought that you'll complete it so quickly.
Don't tell others what you're doing and how you're doing. They don't give a damn about what you do in your own life. Show them results only, don't tell the whole process. As nowadays, people love your failure than your success.
Keep motivating yourself. Give yourself gifts for your progresses or for achieving something.
As,

"It is only you who will be always by your side and will never leave you at any cost, so love yourself as much as you can, because you have to live this whole life on your own."

Tuhina Sharma

Tuhina Sharma is from Jodhpur, Rajasthan. She is studying M.Sc. Zoology from J.N.V. University, Jodhpur. Co-author of two anthologies (Flames of life and Mithaas).

Instagram Handle: @diary_of_untold_feelings_

New Beginning

Rise like the sun,
shine like the stars,
colourful like the rainbow,
happy like the moon,
smile like the flowers,
dance like the wind,
always be like the nature.

Flourishing Mind

"The end" does not mean,
that something is about to end,
it means that something new is about to start,
just as the morning brings the sun when the night is over.

Ankeeta Sahani

"Your Stance may describe your Personality but Your thoughts represents your Character!" -©ankeetaas
Ankeeta Sahani is a short story(Hindi) or Poem(Hindi/ English) writer. She was Honoured as a Young Talent 2020 (In Sambalpur) on the ocassion of Republic day of India. Elder daughter of Mrs. Archana Sahani & Mr. Rajesh Kumar Sahani, Ankeeta hails from Hirakud(Odisha). Ankeeta is a Radio Jockey from Hirakud, Odisha.

Mail id: ommsri242@gmail.com

Instagram Handle: @ankeetaas

सब कुछ हमारे हाथों में है!!

आज भी कुछ गलियों में बिजली के खंबे खड़े नहीं हो पाए हैं। पक्के रास्तों की सुविधा नहीं है। शाम के ६ बजते ही, आज भी कई सारे इलाके सुनसान हो जाते हैं। उसी सुनसान-अंधेरी जगहों पर बहती हवा, डर की हवा होती है। हवा जो चीखती है वहां पर रहने वालों के दोनों कानों में और चिल्लाती रहती है पूरी-पूरी रात!! ना किसी को चैन कि नींद सोने देती है, ना इजाज़त देती है वहां से दूर... बहुत दूर चले जाने को। फिर भी इस सब से किसी भी व्यक्ति को कोई परहेज़ नहीं। उसी चीख-चिल्लाई में आधी रात को गूंजते श्वानों का रोना सुनने के बाद भी जब दूसरे सवेरे सभी लोग वक्त पे नींद से उठ कर अपने-अपने कामों में व्यस्त होना नहीं भूलते, तब ये जाहिर हो जाता है; "ज़िन्दगी बद से बत्तर हो सकती है, लेकिन प्रतिक्रिया कब और किस बात पर दिखाना है, अंत तक हमारे ही हाथों में है।"

Padma Srivastava

She is Padma Srivastava, born and brought up in Varanasi and started writing from her childhood. She is not only writer, she is also fond of singing. Before it she has been co-author of several anthologies. Her first anthology got published in TITLI from flairs and glairs publication. She is a student of Archaeology from Banaras Hindu University. She is nature lover and want to be alone most of the times.

Instagram Handle: @_s_unknown_feelings

मेरी उड़ान

एक मुराद है तुमसे मिलने की
एक ख्वाहिश है तुम संग उड़ने की
न उड़ सकती हूं तुम बिन
न भूलने की हिम्मत ही रखती हूं
पर एक बात तुम लिखकर ले लो ऊचाईयों
प्यार है मुझे तुमसे, बस तभी तक दूर हूँ
जिस दिन तुम जुनून बन गए ना
बेशक तुम्हें मेरे संग चलना ही होगा।।
बेशक है ऊंचाइयों से प्यार मुझे
हां हूँ वाकिफ़ इस बात से भी मैं
ज़्यादा उड़ने वाले सीधे ज़मीं पर आते हैं
पर एक न एक दिन गिरना तो है
सबको ही सांसों से तो क्यूँ न उड़ान भरके गिरे,
क्यूं न शौक पूरे करके गिरे
कम से कम कोई मलाल तो ना रहेगा बाकी
कोई न रहे ना सही
उड़ने में ये ऊंचाई तो रहेगा अपना साथी
हां मंज़ूर है बिल्कुल गिरना मुझे...बशर्ते ऐ ख़ुदा
उड़ान इतनी तो मेरी ज़रुर पूरी होनी चाहिए
कि आसमान जो मुट्ठी में तो भर नहीं सकती
पर कम से कम उसकी ऊंचाइयों का लुत्फ़ तो उठा सकूं
गिरूं, बेशक गिर जाऊँ
पर ख्वाहिशें नहीं अधूरी रहनी चाहिए।।

Adya Kumar

Adya is a student of class 11 and writing for her is like a refreshing cup of coffee and it makes her feel lively. Pouring her heart out onto the paper makes her feel light.

Instagram Handle: @illusionary.tranquility

Hope

It's beautiful how we can do anything with hope. A little believe in yourself and an evergreen smile through all the pains. Yeah what I am saying is scary but what is scarier is not believing in your true potential and worrying about things you can't change. Everyday is a new day and can always be a new beginning if you let it. Forgive yourself for where you went wrong yesterday and take off with new aspirations.

Free Yourself

Like stars that always shine even when they burn inside, you can too just let go things you can't control, give life a chance to take a decision. Give yourself a nudge and then free yourself, live for yourself. Be patient don't conclude easily, you will miss the small details while chasing larger ones. Don't stress yourself about something so far into the future because it will only hurt you. Be strong and don't push for things to happen. Take your time to understand, you will see how things become crystal clear.

Yachika Prajapati

Co-author Yachika Prajapati is a good writer from Haridwar, Uttarakhand. She has completed his intermediate in commerce stream. She has been writing poetry for 8th class April year 2015-16 as her passion. She wants to be a Social Worker in future.

Instagram Handle: @hidden_person_26

ज़िंदगी

जिंदगी को इतना भी गमगीन ना कीजिये,
मुश्किल हज़ारो हो खुल के सामना कीजिये।।

कभी ना रहें बीते दिनों में, न कल की सोचकर आज को अपने खराब कीजिये,
जितना हो सके अपने आज को कल से बेहतर कीजिये।।

फ़लक का चाँद

जिंदगी में हारे हो तो अच्छा काम हुआ है,
तेरा गिरने के बाद ही उठने की हिम्मत से नाम हुआ है।।

किया है जो वक़्त ने कमाल शुक्रिया अदा कर,
तुझे ठोकरो ने ही उस फलक का चाँद किया है।।

Christy Gnana Deepa. J

Christy Gnana Deepa, compiler, writer pursuing her Undergraduate in English literature in Madurai, Tamilnadu, India. She is a compiler of an anthology SECLUDED HEARTS and THE ARDENT HEARTS. Moreover, she is a co-author of more than 25 Anthologies. A writer by passion and a literarian by profession. She is a wattpad and Mirakee writer too. Check her out on instagram as ___budding___writer

Instagram Handle: @___budding___writer

THE INNER ENGINEERING

Accepted the challenge wholeheartedly,
And commenced it carefully,
Ventured the obstacles boldly,
And concluded it perfectly.

Faced the audience proudly,
They greeted me pragmatically,
I thanked them humbly,
Won the given challenge finally.

Quote

Don't wait for tomorrow!
Make today exalted.

Rohan

Rohan is from Ghaziabad, Uttar Pradesh. He is a graduate, works as a cabin crew for an international airline & he really loves writing poetry's, quotes. He is writing from last 4 to 5 years & hope you all will like his work.

Instagram Handle: @roohaniyattttt

दिखने लगा हूँ

अब बातें बोलने से ज़्यादा लिखने लगा हूँ,
पहले छुपा-छुपा रहता था अब थोड़ा दिखने लगा हूँ,
पहले क़ीमत कुछ ना थी मेरी अब हर जगह ऊँची कीमत पर बिकने लगा हूँ,
अब बातें बोलने से ज़्यादा लिखने लगा।।

ज़िद पे अड़ा हूँ

ज़िन्दगी में बहुत-सी मुश्किलों से लड़ा हूँ मैं शायद तभी अपनी उम्र से बड़ा हूँ मैं,
हारना नही चाहता अब किसी भी हालत में बस इसी ज़िद पर अड़ा हूँ मैं...

Abshaar Ibrahim

Abshaar Ibrahim is a medical student, an avid reader and an enthusiastic writer. With an imaginative and creative thought process, she pens down poetries that reflects nature and science. The blend of scientific elements in poetry is a forte she wishes to accomplish. She lives by the philosophy "Your mind believes what you feed it, so feed it Positivity, feed it hope and above all feed it love".

Instagram Handle: @abshaarsaeed

The Virtues of a Scribe

Write until you find yourself
Like the warm sun find it's way through mist
Let all your drafts coalesce into a masterpiece
Like the mighty river absorbing tiny streams
From the darkness of pigments, enlighten the ignorance of soul
Till the sharpness of nib
Blunt the fears untold
Strokes of pen, wings of a butterfly
When flutters at one place,
takes it's effects far and wide
Let the movement of your quill
Be elegant like a swan
Sailing smoothly above
Feet working ferociously till dawn

Write until your words becomes a voice
Of reflections and rejoice
Write until you free yourself
From the constraints of such afflictions
Imposed on self, imposed by others
Glorify your courage on paper with
strongest conviction.
Write until all your tears are soaked
In dried parchment and wet ink
Write until in a world of happiness and ease
Your heart shall sink.

Arya Ojha

Arya Ojha is a poetess. She loves to write and recite poetry. Anchoring, crafting are other combination of her hobbies. She had participated in various anthologies which is going to be released soon. Her instagram handle is @unplugged.soul where she has wonderful piece of write-ups.

उलझे बालों से है कुछ गहरी रिश्तेदारी,
मैगी नाम से जाने ये दुनिया सारी।
लिखना और बोलना ही है इनका दास्तां,
बनारस जैसे खूबसूरत शहर से है इनका वास्ता।

Instagram Handle: @unplugged.soul

The stage of success

Success and Failure,
Two words, great meaning.
Stay devoted,
It will never be raining.
The chaos and hurdle,
It will always go inside.
You need to be great,
To achieve the aim's ride.
Work and work,
You have to work.
No timepass,
That's your mark.
Stay motivated,
That's the only thing you need.
You are a champ,
Because the game of success is abled.

Vishali S.

Vishali was a literature student. She wanna to use all opportunities for her success. She loves her mom to the core. She wanna to travel other countries. She wants to learn many languages. She wants to live herself not like anyone.

Instagram Handle: @visa1_818

Motivational

Once upon a time, there was one girl who lived with her parents in Bihar. She is a curious girl. She always thinking innovative. One day night she came out and saw the nature's beauty at the same time she saw the gorgeous moon. She felt into the beauty of the moon and adore the beauty of the moon. She asked to the moon that you attract all the people of the world, you are charming forever although why you are in the darkness? The moon replied that yeah! I am the beauty of the nature but in morning sun is the big cheese(important person). I am not the beauty of the day time but in the night I am the beauty. Although, I am not beautiful the dark sky makes me gorgeous. So don't worry about you are in the dark because if you're in brightness you will shine means that is not your proud it can't be fame. If you bounce back from the darkness you are the real achiever. You are in darkness although you try to enrich your skills and knowledge to overcome from that struggles. Don't panic to live in darkness try to burn the candle in your life, it becomes bright. The dark part of your life teach you how to reach your destination and also how to face your obstacles in your life.

Moral: Shine in the darkness, you are the brightness of the darkness.

Aasifa Khanam

She have completed her graduation. She have got D.EL.ED degree and now she is trying to become a teacher. She want to be a writer. And she want to give her thinking to the world.

Instagram Handle: @muntazir_khwabeeda

नौकरी वाली बहू

आज मैं एक संवाद का हिस्सा बनी मगर चुप्पी साधे हुए संवाद का शीर्षक "नौकरी वाली बहू" इस संवाद में सारी वार्ता महिलाओं के बारे में थी मगर संवाद में शामिल सभी उम्मीदवार 3 पुरूष और एक महिला थी। एक पुरूष का मानना था महिलाओं को नोकरी इसलिए नही करनी चाहिए क्योंकि फिर उनमें मर्दों के अत्याचार सहने के डर नही रहता और वे मर्दों से बराबरी करने लग जाती हैं। दूसरे मर्द के विचार थे के बहु अगर नौकरी वाली होगी तो घर में नोकरानी नही रहेगी और घर में अशान्ति फेल जाएगी। तीसरा मर्द मानता था के लड़कियों को शिक्षा तो पूरी हाँसिल कर लेनी चाहिए पर नौकरी नही करनी चाहिए। और अंततः जब संवाद में शामिल वो एक मात्र महिला अपने विचार रखने वाली थी तो मुझे लगा चलो कोई तो अब अलग बात निकल कर आएगी परन्तु जब महिला ने विचार रखे तो मैं निःशब्द रह गई.... महिला के विचार थे के बहु को नौकरी इसलिए नहीं करनी चाहिए के अगर वो नौकरी करेगी तो घर को संभालने वाला कोई नहीं रहेगा उनकी सेवा करने वाला कोई नही रहेगा इसलिए उसे नौकरी नही करनी चाहिए। इस संवाद का मैं हिस्सा तो रही मगर कुछ बोल ना सकी क्योंकि वो लोग मानसिक रूप से इस हद तक बीमार थे के मैं अगर उन्हें समझाने जाती तो वो मुझे समझाने लगते। इस पूरे संवाद में इन सब ने मिल कर यह निश्चय कर लिया के एक लड़की को नोकरी करनी चाहिए या नही मगर अफसोस सिर्फ इस बात का है के जिन लड़कियों की बात हो रही थी उनमें से किसी ने नही पूछा के वो क्या चाहती है। किसी ने उसे हक़ नही दिया के जो ज़िन्दगी वो जी रही है किस तरह से जिये, वो नौकरी करना चाहती है या नही उससे किसी ने नही पूछा, उसकी इच्छाओं का गला घोंटते हुए उन लोगो को बिल्कुल अहसास भी नही था।

इस दुनिया में अधिकांश मर्द और औरतें मुर्दा हैं खुशियां मनाओ सब मरते जा रहे हैं कोई विचारों से कोई आज़ादी से।

Sakshi Jain

Co-author Sakshi Jain is a good writer from Hathras. She has completed her diploma and currently pursuing B.tech. She has been writing poetry from 1 year as her passion. She wants to be a self publishing author in future. Follow her writings on instagram and facebook: @_shenu_writings_

अपने शब्दों को कागज़ पर रखती हूँ,
जो कभी कह ना पायी वो दर्द अब मैं लिखती हूँ।।

Instagram Handle: @_shenu_writings_

खुद को पाया है मैंने

काफी लम्बा सफर तय करके ही खुद को पाया है मैने
काफी झूठे रिश्तों का सच जानकर ही खुद को मजबूत बनाया है मैने
मैं जो कभी नही बनना चाहती थी लोगों ने मुझे वो बनाया है
किसी को खुश करने की जरुरत नही है अब मुझे
क्यूंकि अँधेरे में खुद को अकेला पाया है मैनें
वक़्त के साथ बदल जाना ही हक़ीक़त है
ये ही सच अपनाया है मैने
अपनो से ही सबसे ज्यादा दर्द पाया है मैने
और फिर उस वक़्त को भी तो भुलाया है मैने
सबको लेकर चलना तो मुमकिन नही है
इसलिए अब सबसे पीछा छुड़ाया है मैनें
पहले खुद को खोकर ही
आज खुद को पाया है मैनें
मेरे अन्दर की मिनी मी ने मुझे ये ही समझाया है
की तेरा तो कोई था ही नही
एक तूने ही तो बस तेरा साथ निभाया है
जिनको तूने अपना समझा था वो तो बस भरम का एक साया है।

Ankita Mahana

A simple and chirpy girl of 19 who gets inspired from everything that surrounds her and by her observations she loves to weave beautiful bunch of words. She dreams to achieve something to make her parents proud. She's also a firm believer of Karma. Her mirakee ID is "dove_wings".

Instagram Handle: @_the_seraphina_

FREE WINGS

Never feel yourself impotent
Bonded by the chains of limitations;
Remember that you're gifted
With your own pair of heavenly wings;
So always attempt to fly high above all
Assuming the sky as your only limit.

SHINING FOREVER

Let the clouds of negativity come in your way,
They will only make you more sharp and finer;
Remember you're the sun, who'll shine anyway.

NEW IDENTITY

Dream of a life ahead of
All these taunts by the society;
Make yourself stand out so much so that
You never need to introduce yourself further;
And let the crowd cheer out your name.

STOP NEVER

Try to flourish among the thorns
Like the roses;
Try to bloom amidst the mud
Like the lotuses;
Try to shine among the stars
Like the moon;

Because,

Unsuitable circumstances
Are not the permanent barriers
Against our dreams;
We all have the capability
To rise from all odds;
And just move on till we reach
Our actual destination...

Shivani M.R. Joshi

Co-author Shivani is a good writer from Ahmedabad, Gujarat. She is only 20 years old. She has completed her Education in science stream. She has been writing poetry for last six months as her passion. For the past some days, she has been published among the people in the form of a writer, she write many encouraging stories and many poems and some of her writings has been printed in many books. She wants to be a doctor in future.

Instagram Handle: @shivanijoshi271

कारण चाहे कुछ भी हो

कारण चाहे कुछ भी हो रोने का फिर भी तुम मुस्कुराओ,
कारण चाहे कुछ भी हो उदासी का फिर भी तुम खुश रहो,
कारण चाहे कुछ भी हो नाकामयाबी का तुम फिर से शुरू करो,
कारण चाहे कुछ भी हो जिंदगी मे परेशान होने का फिर भी तुम मजे से उसे जिया करो।

कहने से कुछ नहीं होता

कहने से कुछ नहीं होता कुछ करके दिखाना होता है,
बैठे रहने से कुछ नहीं होता मैदान में आना पड़ता है,
कुछ बनने के लिए आराम की छांव से निकलकर धूप में तड़पना पड़ता है,
तब जाकर कोई इंसान शख्सियत बनता है।

Sanjay Naik

Sanjay Naik is from Kharagpur State of West Bengal. He is an Economics graduate (Hons), a writer from the heart and passionate about singing. Through the platform of anthology, he wants to spread love & positivity among his readers and wants to heal his readers' hearts with his magical words. Sanjay is at utmost peace when he pens his emotions. He believes that the power of his words, will heal the wounds of many readers.

Instagram Handle: @the_poetry_wo

Flight --- "Air Hostess"

I have kept my spirits high
touching the sky will be my pride
There are many aspirations left now
My courage will be the same at every step.

I will keep flying my dreams in anticipation
I will have an identity on the stairs of success
I have a hold of many languages
It will be a little easier for me to talk.

I take care of the convenience of different passengers
I will have a smile on my face at all times
I have the courage to handle the responsibilities
Even in the worst of circumstances
my courage will be patient.

I am fond of turning dreams into reality
one day time will be my Slave
I am the little bird of my father & mother
They would be proud of me.

Isha B Vaghela

Isha is a developing author. She is 18 years old. She studies in SV-NIT Surat under Chemical engineering department. She loves to write to songs. Her poems are the way she speaks about and for her emotions. Her hobbies are to write, to dance, to listen to the music. You can follow her on Instagram id: isha_vaghela02.

Instagram Handle: @isha_vaghela02

Ignore oblivion

Day would come one
Shall I have business none
Would have I captured some
Words calibrated to run
Over the entire sun.

Feminism

There she goes, with a shining smile.
Staring eyes at her flourishing light.
So much says her icy eyes,
Still what makes so much sense to her,
Is the only thing she longed for the most.

Arundhati Shekar

Arundhati Shekar is a co-author and a student by designation who is pursuing her graduation in commerce and Company Secretarialship. She started to write when she was 17 years old and the passion continued, as of now she has written about 250 poems, she mostly writes about self love, love, friendship, confidence. She has an audience of about 800 people on Instagram and most of her poems are related by all of them.

Instagram Handle: @__tale_of_hearts_

Darkness to enlightenment

Desires are the flames in my heart,
which is taking me to the destiny I deserve,
I know, this is just a story to the world,
for me this is a soothing memory for a lifetime;

how immature was I,
crying and blaming so hard,
thinking if the struggles were worth the time,
and the dreams were worth time;

my existence was then being questioned,
it was actually confusing just like a puzzle,
what would I do, I could barely talk about it then,
because, I knew you wouldn't have believe me then;

my journey of success was never that easy,
so do the spark of my dreams,
finally achieved what I always wanted to,
so cheers to the hard work and consistency which never let me sleep;

The strange strengths

I found time to focus on myself,
not when I was alone,
but when I was amidst people,
I got to love myself more,
not when the people were favourable around,
but when I was surrounded by the people I barely knew,
the struggles were all worth it,
they helped me know my worth,
they helped me find the sparkle within,
they helped me grow,
they created me;

Deepshikha Nathawat

इनका नाम दीपशिखा नाथावत है। ये गुजरात के वडोदरा शहर में अपने बेटे के साथ रहती है। इन्हें बचपन से ही लिखने का शौक है। ये जब 14 साल की थी तब से लिखना शुरू किया। इन्हें लिखने के साथ-साथ संगीत सुनने का और उसे गुनगुनाना बहुत अच्छा लगता है। ये एक केमिकल कंपनी में कार्यालय सहायक के रूप में काम करती है।

Instagram Handle: @deepshikha.nathawat9

काम का पहला दिन

सुनो काम्रेड,
काम का पहला दिन उठी झटपट जल्दी से काम निपटाया
जल्दी में आधे घंटे पहले पहुँच गयी मुझको तनिक ना भाया..
चहल कदमी करी थोड़ी सी फिर फोन से बातों में वक्त बिताया
मैम को जब फोन किया तो उनका इंतजार का फरमान आया..
नयी जगह नया काम समझने में मैने जरा ना समय लगाया
जल्दी-जल्दी काम किया तब नींद के झोकों ने बडा़ सताया..
दफ्तर छूटा पहुँची घर पर वहाँ ट्यूशन के बच्चों ने शोर मचाया
कैसे-कैसे प्रसंग हुए अब हंस-हंस के सभी सखियों को बताया
कितना मुश्किल है पैसे कमाना मुझको ये झोल समझ अब आया
काम का पहला दिन था मेरा देखो मैनें ऐसे भागदौड़ में बिताया।

नाम में क्या रखा है?

काम ही तेरी पहचान बने ऐसा तू नाम कर
तेरे चेहरे से सच झलके ऐसा तू काम कर
नाम में क्या रखा है?
तेरे वजूद को ही तेरी सूरत से पहचाने सब
अपना सर झुकाए वो देखे तुझको कोई जब
नाम में क्या रखा है?
चमके तेरा ललाट तू ऐसा तेरा अभिमान रख
रहे तेरे सभी तलबगार ऐसा तेरा सम्मान रख
नाम में क्या रखा है?

Gunjan Jogia

Gunjan Jogia from Porbandar, Gujarat is a homemaker and a mother of two lovely kids. She completed her graduation from IGNOU. Her passion for reading inspired her to write her unexpressed thoughts into words…

Instagram Handle: @gunjavinodi

उड़ान

अपने ख्वाबों से,
उठकर देखो,
ये सारा जहाँ तुम्हारा है।
उड़ान भरो पंछियों वाली,
फिर तूम देखो,
ये सारा आसमान तुम्हारा है।

समुद्र

मन के भीतर बसे,
दुःखों की लहरें बनाकर किनारों पे फेंक दो।
ढूंढो तो सुख यहीं है,
सुख की लहरों को अपने अंदर समेट लो।
खुद को गहराई से स्थिर करो।
समुद्र जैसे ही शांत बनो।

गलती

माना और सुधारा जाए,
तो गलती वरदान है,
नकारा और दोहराया जाए,
तो गलती अभिशाप।

सूरज

ढलता सूरज,
कुछ संदेश देके अस्त होता है।
उगता सूरज,
नई दिशाओं के साथ उदय होता है।

Sirisha Susarla

Sirisha is a psychologist by profession, she is very passionate about writing poetry and is a published author. She strongly believes that words are people's best friends and poetry is the relationship between words and the writer.

Instagram Handle: @sirisha_susarla

When I am all alone: Tale of feelings

Just when I thought it's all right...life said turn left. I was all alone on my own, mixed feelings with so many emotions running, I almost had hit rock bottom, and all this while I invested a lot of time in thinking who's there for me and who's not, until I realised the most important question I should ask myself is that am I there for myself? Because there are people who genuinely care about what happens to me but they can't leave their lives and lift me up by being physically around, mentally they have been there always so I need to take charge, I have to be there and bounce back, self reflection is very important when you are low, figuring out life isn't easy and nobody ever said it's gonna be easy either....just now as I write this, I have tears in my eyes but is this how I am gonna feel forever? No! Change is constant and we must go with it, life is a lot more than what we think about it. I decided to not let myself down, I choose to lift myself up, I'll get there one step at a time.

Life As It Is!

Life is as spontaneous as this write-up of mine, I came across this opportunity to write and I didn't have a lot of time to actually think and write something very deep. I then suddenly realised that writing about success, positivity and motivation has nothing to do with structure but with your own experiences.

I think to succeed in life, one must look at life as it is. We should not try to mend the flow, we should not compare it with that of others because it's your life, your story, your struggle and most importantly your happiness. I hope this write-up finds you well and I wish everyone reading this out there looks at life and accepts it for what it is, give life a fair deal and you will see yourself loving it completely.

Sahina Ghugha

Sahina Ghugha is 20 year old B.Com student at Saurashtra university Rajkot. She is from Jamnagar city of Gujarat. She is state level winner in poetry competition 2017. She is Co-author of 10+ anthologies. She is an amazing writer and poet and she wants do something for society through her pen.

Instagram Handle: @itz_sahina_write

कश्ती

तूफ़ानों से निकल गई है कश्ती,
मंज़िल पर पहुँचना अभी बाकी है।
विवश हूं परिस्थिति के आगे,
ललकारना इनको अभी बाकी है।

न पूछिए ये परिस्थिति मुझे कैसे रंग दिखलाई है।
गैरो ने सहारा दिया, अपनों से ठोकर खाई है।
समय तुम्हारा था, अब हमारा होगा,
समय में बदलाव लाना अभी बाकी है।
विवश हूं परिस्थिति के आगे,
ललकारना इनको अभी बाकी है।

अनुभव मेरी उम्र नहीं, परिस्थिति मुझे दिलाई है।
पाठशाला से बेहतर, जीवन का ज्ञान सिखाई है।
अंधेरे में बिखरी है सुबह मेरी,
उसे समेट लाना अभी बाकी है।
विवश हूं परिस्थिति के आगे,
ललकारना इनको अभी बाकी है।

Ankita Bhatia

Ankita Bhatia hailing from New Delhi, working as Immigration Consultant in real world and entrepreneur in virtual world. Co-author and compiler of 10+ anthologies and blogger @_purposeoflife_by_ankita on Instagram.

Instagram Handle: @_purposeoflife_by_ankita and @_anthologies_by_ankita

Success in my veins

Surely am in love with success
Where the best hug is of achievements
Moving and Moving with all my zeal
To prove them wrong
Who underestimated my power
And make my parents proud
Who supported me all around
Moving and moving with all my zeal
Because I see My goals welcoming me....
Surely am in love with success
And love is blind
and So is I in love of success.

Joydeep Mallik

Joydeep Mallik is from Agartala, Tripura. He is studying English (B.A. Hons) at MBB College. His hobbies are playing cricket, harmonium, writing quotes and poems based on love and heartbreak content. At first, he started writing quotes casually, but after a while, he got motivation from his closest friend. After getting motivation from her, he started writing more and more. Her words of motivation, motivated him to write quotes even further and after a while it became a passion to him.

Instagram Handle: @lovesque.quotes.writer

Success and its Connotation

Someone: Success!
What "Success" really mean?

I replied: Hmm! Success!!
When you see your close ones or loved ones smile and happiness due to your deeds, this is actual success.

And,
When you make them proud of you,
this is what really mean, to be
True Success.

Sanoj Kumar

He is an engineer, started writing two years back never imagined that people would like it, and feel his emotions as theirs. He also likes to express other's feelings and always try to change other's mindsets in a better way through his writings. Nowadays, he is a member of many writing communities and earned lots of certificates through his writings. His first book as an author named "सफ़र, जिन्दगी का" and he also works on many anthologies as compiler and editor. Currently, he is a co-author approx 50 anthologies. If you want to know more then simply type safarzindagikask in Google.

Blog: http://safarzindagikask.blogspot.com
Email: thehiddenwritersk@gmail.com

Instagram: @the_hidden_writer_sk

मेहनत कर

ओये यारा तू कहां खो गया,
अपनी हंसी, मुस्कुराहट किसे दे दिया।
मुश्किल परिस्थिति का सामना करते-करते,
कहीं तूने भी तो अपने घुटने ना टेक दिया।

चल बहुत हुआ, अब तू जवाब दे,
तूने क्या किया, खुद को हिसाब दे।
यूहीं मेहनत कर पीछे ना हटा कर,
तू हार नहीं माने हो, ये सब को बता दे।

क्या हुआ वक़्त तुझसे नाराज़ है,
अपने कठिन परिश्रम से उसे भी मना ले।
ऐसे समय में ताना मारने के वजाय साथ दे,
ये अपनों के साथ-साथ सबको समझा दे।

कुछ नया करने में वक़्त लगता है,
खुद रास्ते बना कर चलना आसान कहां है।
अगर सफल हो गए अपने बनाए मुकाम पर,
तब तो दुनियां में उससे बेहतर जहान कहां है।

Sakshi Jain

She is Sakshi Jain from Roorkee, Uttarakhand pursuing BA Sociology. She is a decent child. She is the Co-author in around 150 anthologies and currently working as a Compiler in around 4 anthologies. She is the hard-working girl. Her Instagram handle is @sakshijain_writes.

Instagram Handle: @sakshijain_writes

Think Twice

You might be right
Think for 2 and half minutes about your life
and what you have done with it and what
you still can do with it.
what if I told you people who said "yes" also failed many,
maybe even more than you.
What if I told you that your life is just around the corner.
What if you read this and decided to change your life for
better?
What if you decided to make it
Whatever you are going through
Whatever you think is holding you
back you abolish it and don't let it tear you apart? again!!
what if you…
what if you tried just one more time?
gave it one more shot?

Jeevitha. S

She is a girl with stupendous writing skills. Her heart is a castle abound with unbreakable courage, being contained with enticing dreams. Penning is her way of spreading aesthetic vibes among her readers. Being a literarian is her pride. She loves to be a unicorn amidst the flock of sheep's!

Instagram Handle: @_jeevitha_sundar_

Unflinching belief upon life!

Although she walked through her darkest days,
She always had a glimmer in her eyes.
She believed in something which was unseen and unheard,
That one thing was her hope on the whole;
She edified something new in all that she went through,
She became aesthetic on the whole,
Miracle does happen at the end;
When she rejuvenated her soul through her hope.
There exists the glide of positive vibes,
She summoned more wisdom and insight.
All her dejections flew away;
And her eyes once again shimmered with jubilance.
Accepting struggles and proceeding further more,
Her puzzles were solved through her beliefs upon life.

Vaishnawi Kumari

Vaishnawi Kumari is from Patna, Bihar. She is studying in B.Tech from NSIT Bihta. Her hobbies are singing, dancing and writing. She didn't write to become a writer, she writes to share her feelings and she motivated and supported by her father.

Instagram Handle: @kumarivaishnawi

बिन परिश्रम फल कहा...?

जानती हूँ बड़े कोमल हैं तुम्हारे पांव
कांटे सह नहीं सकते...
मगर कहते हैं न
"बिना पेड़ लगाए फल खा नहीं सकते"
कुछ मंजिलों को पाने के लिए
पांवों में कांटे चुभोने पड़ते हैं...
हर एक मंजिल आसानी से मिल
जाए बार -बार वो खुशनसीब हो नहीं सकते...
खुदा भी देखता है मेहनत और
सिद्दत सबकी वो भी कहते हैं
"जितना करोगे उतना पाओगे"
किसी मेहनती के साथ
नाइंसाफी वो कर नहीं सकते...

विश्वास हैं हमे

कैसे कहते हो हमसे ना हो पाएगा
कोशिश करोगे तो मंजिल भी हाथ आएगा...
माना मुश्किलें बहुत हैं राहों में
लेकिन खुद को कैसे साबित कर पाओगे...
मेहनत करते हैं हम फल वो देते हैं
हर मुश्किलों से लड़कर आगे बढ़ाते हैं...
हाँ... जानती हूँ मन उदास हैं तुम्हारा
एक बार कि गई कोशिश हर बार रंग नहीं लाती
बार बार कोशिश करो सफलता हाथ जरूर आएगी...
विश्वास है हमें तुमपे
तुम मंजिल जरूर पाओगे...
रूको नहीं बढ़ते चलो
राहें-ए-मंजिल कदम चुम चाएगी....

Sushmita Mishra

She is a government teacher with multiple skills like writing, dancing, painting, etc. Now, she is a youtuber also. So, she spread her creative skills with others through youtube.

Instagram Handle: @kuch.to.logkaheng

मै ज़िन्दगी के हर रंग को जीना चाहती हूँ...

मै ज़िन्दगी के हर रंग को जीना चाहती हूँ
सिर्फ चमकदार बिना दाग वाला
सफेद पन्ना ही नहीं
बल्कि काला लाल पीला गुलाबी
हर रंग के सच से रूबरू होना चाहती हूँ
मै ज़िन्दगी के हर...
जैसे तितलियाँ उड़ती हैं ना
ढ़ेर सारे रंगों को एक साथ समेटे
बंद कली से खिले फूल तक
ठीक वैसे ही मै भी हर उपवन में
फिरना चाहती हूँ..
लेकिन सिर्फ खिले फूलों की नहीं बल्कि
बेजान, मुरझाये फूलों की खुशबू भी
महसूस करना चाहती हूँ
मै ज़िन्दगी के हर...
जैसे चिड़ियाँ चहकती हैं,
दूर खुले आसमानों मे, ठीक वैसे ही मै भी
ढेर सारी ख्वाहिशों को अपने आँचल मे समेटे...
बहुत दूर उस गगन मे जाना चाहती हूँ
लेकिन सिर्फ खुले आसमान मे ही नहीं
बल्कि जमीं पर बसी अनदिखी
संकरी गलियों से भी गुज़रना चाहती हूँ
मै ज़िन्दगी के हर...
जैसे नदियाँ बहती हैं ना किसी कोने से
कल कल की धुन के साथ
वैसे ही मै भी एकांत में रहना चाहती हूँ
लेकिन सिर्फ अपने ही मन की धुन नहीं
बल्कि ज़िन्दगी के हर सुर को सुनना चाहती हूँ...

मै ज़िन्दगी के हर रंग...
जैसे एक चित्रकार तस्वीर को
अपने मनचाहे रंगों से सजाता है ना...
ठीक वैसे ही मै भी अपनी तस्वीर सजाना चाहती हूँ
लेकिन सिर्फ अपनी पसंद के रंगों से नहीं
बिना भेदभाव के दुनिया के हर रंग से
उसको रंगना चाहती हूँ
मै जिंदगी के हर रंग को जीना चाहती हूँ...

Nivetha R C

Nivetha R C, a young poetess from Coimbatore, Tamil Nadu. She graduated BA English Literature from PSGR Krishnammal College for Women, Coimbatore. Currently, she is pursuing MA English in KSG College of Arts and Science, Coimbatore. She started writing poems from the age of 13. She used to write in Tamil and English. Nivetha likes to personify the things around her and tries to reveal its emotions through her words. She is interested to deliver the unheard conversations between two non-living things. She likes to write poems with rhyming words. Sometimes she uses to write acrostic poems too.

Instagram Handle: @if_pen_could_talk

Unheard Conversation

I don't think I will be able to achieve
"You will succeed if you start to believe"
Everywhere I go I end up facing insults
"Start working, shortly you will see the results"
To be frank I don't know how to start
"Think think your way is not apart"
No one is there to support my back
"Self-confidence is what you lack"
Though I am ready everyone is teasing
"Your actions can make them freezing"
I am so scared to face a setback
"Experience of failure is your backpack"
Why are you talking to me? I am so reserved
"Your Antagonist I am, Hope is what I served."

A conversation between Self-doubt and Self-belief.

'Grace' = Positivity

"A little plant thinks one day a flower will bloom
With hope, it will happen soon
Every other day it is blessed with sunray
It thinks there comes the way
By seeing the stars it tells the wish
The next day rain placed a kiss
Other plants mocking made its heart to get a scar
All this will end soon it was aware
One day a little girl entered the place
And named the little plant as 'Grace'
Every day the plant took the positive vibes
From the words the little girl describes
One day the plant reached its destiny
Not with a single flower but plenty buds shiny".

Yes, Grace to its next folk, showed what is hope.

Kareena Verma

She is Kareena Verma the Daughter of Mr. Kehru Verma and Mrs. Rajeshwari Verma and She is a computer science student currently pursuing the Bachelor of Computer application, she has been writing since one year and a co-author of many Anthology and same as her name Kareena delineate alike her name, sanguine with her soul, pure with her heart, innocent with her straightforward thoughtful perceptions!

For her Rectitude within her is everything & nothing is above than Viracity with our nation, she wants only to flame alike terracotta Diya, for one day she'll spread the happiness of lights as the most bright star in the sky of someone home and just wanna to spread love of humanity every where!!

Instagram Handle: @warrior_thephoenix_birdie

Happiness with prosperity

Everyday to search happiness wisely
Start your day with more challenging nicely
Someday will be you are going to very down
But don't feel Agonizing, stop everything and just shutdown
Judgmental society made you thrush,
But you must have to stand up,
Don't troublemaker & haven't collapse
Victory is not only about Name, Fame and wealthy life,
It's also meant to be serving of joying in some happiness life
But trust me, you must have to believe in yourself,
Be patience, be calm & god with us when you are too lone but
Never try to be give up anymore in life!

Dear me

The life is full of find fault within me,
Every time the pain inside me,
People won't let you live,
People won't let you laugh,
But they're always be trying to see you
In terrible nights,
People won't let you live,
But wanna see you in trauma!
But the sufferings pains inside you,
Made you solid by heart!
The heart said to you,
Be braveness within you!
Won't let you fall front of the stormy!
And the life has taught you,
The fearless girl inside you!

Gaurav Sharma

Gaurav Sharma is a shayar and co-author of 7 book and he is from Kaman Bharatpur. He is presuming B.A. LLB from Amity University Jaipur.

Instagram Handle: @gauravsharma3832

सकारात्मक्ता

सकारात्मक सोच रखोगे तो सब काम आसान हो जाएंगे
सकारात्मक रही सोच तो आप महान हो जाएंगे
सकारात्मक सोच रखो तो मंज़िल भी मिल ही जाती है
और कोशिश की जाए तो दीवार भी हिल ही जाती है वैज्ञानिकों ने
तूफान को नापने का उपकरण बनाया है
यह सकारात्मक सोच ही तो है जिसने ये कर दिखाया है
सकारात्मक सोच से तो दुनिया भी बदली जा सकती है
और 60% वाले कि भी अच्छी रैंक आ सकती है
सकारात्मक सोच से मिल जाते है समस्या के सब हल
फिर हमेसा करोगे आज, कभी ना कहोगे ये करूँगा कल
परीक्षा खराब जाए तो कोई भी निराशा ना हो
अगला अच्छा हो बस यही आशा होनी चाहिए
देखो प्रयास हर बार करूँगा
पिछली गलतियों में सुधार करूँगा।

Krishna Motwani

Krishna Motwani is a student currently. She use to pen down her feelings. She is a moody girl. She started writing in the month of June, 2020. She writes in her free time. She writes some motivational quotes or poetries too and practices artworks also. She lives her life like a bird As bird flies freely and enjoys life like that she also lives her life freely and enjoy fullest. For motivating and inspiring poems and quotes, you can check her on Instagram.

Instagram Handle: @unique__blog_

Inspires ownself!

I was in love with my classmate. He too was in love with me. We both were in relationship. One of his friend told him that i am doing bluff with him. But no! I was in true love.

Only and only due to bad thinking of his friend or may be due to misunderstanding, he left me. He is too apart from me now. I taken more than 8 months to forget all our memories spent together, to overcome with that dark phase, to forget his smile which always inspires me and much more things.

But now i am motivated, i moved ahead. Life taught a big lesson this time. I was broken inside but now i am bold, i forgot all the memories and everything!! This dark face taught me that life gives problems to make us more stronger. And this thought made me strong, made me bold. I used to cry for him, to call him but no he hadn't taken a single call. Now all those things i forgot, those feelings don't comes again in my mind. A single misunderstanding taught me too much!

Nafisha Mullick

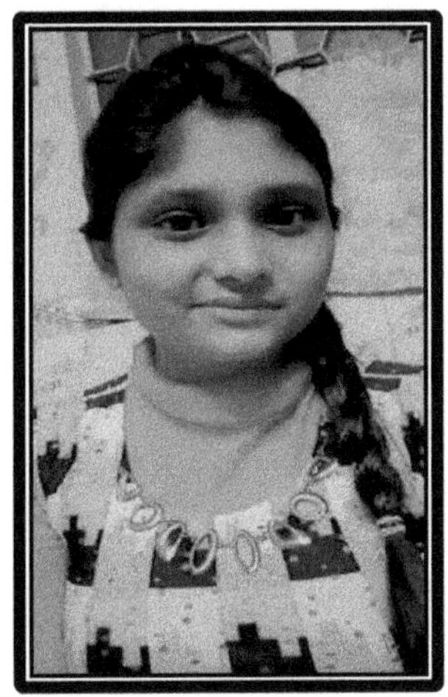

Nafisha Mullick is from city of joy, Kolkata. She is pursuing her graduation in 3rd year (English Honours). She has participated in 20+ writing competitions. She is a passionate writer and loves to pen her thoughts and feelings through her writings.

Instagram Handle: @soulof_december

I Stand witness

I stand witness to the world where people changes there colour everyday more faster than the camelian does…friend turns to enemy...lover falls in love with someone else...but if you earn one dollar it remains one dollar only so make money be independent so that people who used to laugh at you and used to say "you are good for nothing" should one day give you respect, smile for your success and can say "NO OTHER PERSON IS AS BETTER AS YOU".

Believe in yourself

When life gives you Hundred reasons to cry show life that you have thousand reasons to smile. When you feel helpless think that nothing in this world is impossible. Don't remember the wrong deeds of your past but remember the lessons you got from them. Be your own inspiration and create your own fate.

Shubhashish Ranjan

शुभाशीष रंजन जमालपुर (बिहार) से एक बेहतरीन कवि हैं। उन्हें SR36 के एक पेन नाम के साथ रोमांटिक और प्रेरक कविताएं/उद्धरण लिखने का शौक है। आप उनकी इंस्टाग्राम आई.डी. @ranjanshubhashishish और YourQuote आई.डी. Shubhashish Ranjan पर जाकर उनकी कविताओं/उद्धरण का एक मजा ले सकते हैं। शुभाशीष रंजन आपकी मांग पर भी कविताएं/उद्धरण लिख सकते है।

E-mail: shubhashishishranjansr36@gmail.com

Instagram Handle: @ranjanshubhashish

चाहत

ये है उस लड़के की कहानी,
जो लिख रहा इसे अपनी जुबानी।
शुरू से ही ये रहता है शांत,
नहीं पता क्यूँ, पर इसे पसंन्द है एकांत!
बचपन से ही इसे बस आगे रहना था,
नहीं पता क्या पर इसे दुनिया से कुछ तो कहना था।
पापा मम्मी का था ये राज दुलारा,
एक लड़की का था ये आशिक़ आवारा।
किसी कारण वश वो रिश्ता टूट गया!
उन दोनों का साथ बीच में ही छूट गया!
मानो जैसे की वो लूट गया।
कुछ पल के लिए वो खुदसे ही रूठ गया!
अहसास हुआ उसे,अब तो जागना होगा,
अब व्यक्ति के पीछे नही,
बल्कि सपनों के पीछे भागना होगा,
कर लिया उसने उस दिन ही इरादा,
नहीं देगा महत्त्व किसी को खुद से ज्यादा।
आएगा वो भी दिन जब ये दुनिया पर छायेगा,
जितना इसने चाहा है उससे तोह कई ज्यादा पायेगा।

त्याग

त्याग दो वो सारी चीज़े,
जो तुम्हारी कामयाबी के बीच आ रही!
भूल जाओ हर उस इंसान को,
जिनकी यादें, आपको हर दिन खा रही!

जीवन में आये हो तोह मिलेंगे हज़ारों लोग,
हर किसी से बिछड़ने का, कितना करोगे आखिर शोक?

जिसे तुम पा ही सकते थे,
देखना उसके लिए सपना कैसा?
जो इंसान तुम्हें मुसीबत में छोड़ दे,
वो इंसान ही अपना कैसा?

Keerthana Suriya

She is Ms. KEERTHANA SURIYA a highly aspired, dynamic medical student, social-worker, a passionate writer and classical dancer who is engaging in self and social development, building relationships and exhibiting integrity. She is Co-author of various other anthologies. She is Founder of WACHC Foundation- Women And Children Health Care and also holding the position of Women's Health Empowerment Project Head in the trust Women's Renaissance Centre. She strongly believes that "When women and children rise, their communities and countries rise with them". Follow her on Instagram.

Instagram Handle: @keethusm

MAKE IT HAPPEN

Focus
Focus on your goal
Focus on the one person who can
make a real difference in your life.
That is YOU
Remember, there is a power
in what you think and what you say
To achieve your dreams,
you have to take care of yourself.
You have to take care of both
your thoughts and your words.
NOTHING JUST HAPPENS
To be successful you have to work on it.
You have to put effort
Don't be just a hearer. Be a doer
Your action will bring your dreams to reality
I repeat!
NOTHING JUST HAPPENS
YOU HAVE TO MAKE IT HAPPEN.

Aman Siddiqui

अमन सिद्दिकी लेखन कार्य में रुचि रखने के कारण समय-समय पर वतर्मान स्थिति पर अपनी लेखनी के माध्यम से युवाओं को जागरुक करते रहते हैं। इनके द्वारा लिखित पुस्तक 'सफलता के सिद्धांत' है। अलीगढ़ उत्तर प्रदेश में रहते हैं। इनकी प्रारम्भिक शिक्षा शारीरिक विकलांगता के कारण घर पर ही पूर्ण हुई। इसके पश्चात् स्नातक की शिक्षा धरम समाज डिग्री कॉलेज, अलीगढ़ से पूर्ण की। वर्तमान समय में यह एक आई०टी० कम्पनी में कंटेंट राइटर व वेब डेवलपर हैं।

Instagram Handle: @mramansiddiqui

रिश्ते और सफलता

सफलता क्या है? क्या दौलतमंद ही सफल होते हैं? क्या एक गरीब कभी सफल नहीं हो सकता?
खुद से पूछिये कि आपको क्या पाना है और क्या बनना है। यदि आपको अपने मन के मुताबिक जो मिल गया है या जो बन गए हैं क्या आप उससे संतुष्ट हैं? यदि 'नहीं' तो आप अभी भी सफल नहीं हैं। सफलता का अर्थ सिर्फ धन इकट्ठा करना नहीं है। आपके पास बहुत दौलत है लेकिन किसी भी कारण स्वयं को संतुष्टि नहीं है तो आप खुद को सफल नहीं कह सकते हैं।
दौलतमंद होना और सफल होना ये दोनो अलग-अलग पहलू हैं। सफलता तो एक एहसास है जिसका आनंद आपसी रिश्तों के साथ मिलकर लिया जाना चाहिए। आज की भागदौड़ की ज़िंदगी में हम अपने रिश्तों को समय नहीं दे पा रहे हैं । यही कारण है कि हम आज अपनी ख़ुशियों में भी अकेले ही नज़र आते हैं।
बिना बेहतर रिश्तों के हम कभी सफल नहीं कहला सकते हैं। हम जो भी करते हैं ख़ुशी पाने के लिए करते हैं। ख़ुशी हो या ग़म इसे अपनो के साथ ही साझा किया जाता है इसलिए अपने रिश्तों को भी समय दीजिए।
एक अमीर व्यक्ति समाज के लिए सफल हो सकता है, क्यांकि हम इंसान अमीर व्यक्ति की सफलता उसकी दौलत के आधार पर तय करते हैं। सोचते हैं कि उसको क्या कमी उसके पास तो बहुत-सी दौलत है। लेकिन मैं सिर्फ समाज की नज़रों में सफल दिखना, सफलता नहीं मानता। सफलता की अनुभूति तो स्वयं खुद के अन्दर से आनी चाहिए। कितनी ही दौलत हमारे पास क्यों न हो जब तक हमें आत्मसंतुष्टि नहीं मिलती तब तक हमें सफलता की अनुभूति नहीं होती है। क्योंकि अगर सफलता को दौलत से जोड़ कर देखेंगे तो हम कभी सफल नहीं हो सकते, क्योंकि हमारी इच्छाओं का कोई अंत नहीं है।

Darshan Patel

Here by Darshan Patel physiotherapist, co-author who writes about life and with the aim to inspire a one and motivate to those who loose their hope in life and also about that fact of life. A true inspiration from chaanakya niti, bhagwat geeta, santram saurabh, social media, and learning lessons from ones life.

Instagram Handle: @d.2p3

.

Way to success

Way to success
Teacher is a way to reach Heaven.
It is what we can not buy but can learn.
A way by which one can reach the Everest.
Teacher wants his student to spread his ray like sun.
We have to search for a good and true teacher.
Who guide us in every sphere of life.
There are people who utilized us but,
teacher never think of it.
A true teacher will take the student,
to climb the top position in the world!
It's a teacher who is putting
all efforts behind his student.
But nowadays Eklavya is hard to be found!
One who would give all things,
belonging to him to his guru.
Teacher wants his student to become something in future he will feel proud of it.
It's a teacher who gives confidence to the students.
Teacher is our Guiden book, Inspiration and
I don't have a word for him.
I will love and miss them as the days pass by!
To my teachers and principal my guiding torch.
My undying gratitude for all.

Ambition

Ambition is contrast,
As pumping as heart,
Which is not going to take the name of stoping!
Jumping to and fro like a monkey.
Each atom of universe has different ambition.
It is not to achieve Everest in the future,
But a scope of scanning something,
Ambition is never the less nothing.
For bagger to fill his hunger bagging is his aim,
For middle to full fill needs of molecules,
For richers to be Rich! Rich! Rich is his aim,
Each atom of molecules is fill with electrons.

Harshita Verma

Co-author Harshita Verma is a good writer from Lucknow. She has completed her graduation in commerce stream. She has been writing poetry for 6 months as her passion. She wants to be a novelist in future.

Instagram Handle: @0___hsh

THE PATH CHOSEN

A flower growing in a desert
inspires to grown even though lonely.
An ant climbing a mountain
motivates to achieve great heights.
A river flowing among mountains
challenges to reach the goals.
A lamp burning in the darkness
provides hope to fulfill dreams
The hardships faced in life
Make us stronger day by day.
As the path less walked on is the path full of thorns.
This path whenever chosen
ensures success and happiness in life.

HOPE TO BE HAPPY

Leave the dark days behind
Hope the coming days will bring light.
Walk ahead without any fear
Because everything will eventually become clear.
Do not suffer because of past
Because that has been long gone.
Welcome the new days of life
With utmost gleam and happiness.
Pursue your goals with hope
Because they are the one's that will make you happy forever.
Be positive as that's the only rule to be happy in the world full of sufferings.

Ayushman Majhi

He is AYUSHMAN MAJHI from Odisha. An extremely talented and charming boy with immense excellence in the field of Music, Writing and Anchoring. He has received many awards in the field of Music, Writing and Anchoring. He is also felicitated with "The Best Speaker/Anchor 2020" by FCP Excellence Award 2020.

Instagram Handle: @ayushman_majhi

The ultimate motivation for the life

The number of times you break,
The number of times you regain your strength,
To fight with those situations,
Which brought up your anger and aggression,
Never go according to what people say,
Because people are born to say,
But you are born to do something extremely big,
Never give someone's example to anyone,
Rather be an example for everyone,
Never doubt on yourself for all the rest,
Just prove that you are the best,
Don't get afraid when you are alone,
As you are going to create history,
And that's not done by everyone,
That's only done by the specific ones,
Never fear to death,
Because it's not in your hands,
Never fear to anyone,
As you're the strongest among everyone,
Don't run behind anyone,
Just do endless hard work,
Achieve the grand success,
Then the whole world will run behind you.

Muskan Sachdeva

Muskan Sachdeva hails from Basti, Uttar Pradesh. She completed studies from St. Basil's and is pursuing Chartered accountant along with B.Com from Allahabad university. Writing was just a time pass earlier but then it became her passion. She has been co-authored in 25+ anthologies.

Instagram Handle: @muskurate_shabd

समय की कीमत

साल की कीमत उस शख्स से पूछिए, जो फेल हुआ हो
महीने की कीमत उस शख्स से पूछिए, जिसे पिछले महीने की सैलरी ना मिली हो
हफ्ते की कीमत उस शख्स से पूछो, जो पूरा हफ्ता हॉस्पिटल में रहा हो
रोटी की कीमत उससे पूछिए, जो दिन भर से भूखा हो
घंटे की कीमत उससे पूछिए, जिसने किसी का इंतज़ार किया हो
मिनट की कीमत उससे पूछिए, जिसने ट्रेन मिस की हो
सेकंड की कीमत उससे पूछिए, जो दुर्घटना से बाल-बाल बचा हो।

Debesh Prusty

Debesh lays the foundation for his books by describing his experience in the graduation. Although he loves writing microtales from his college life but it is the first time he stepped in to this spot light. Everyone called him an over thinker which made him to write. Even he is too moody, writing is his constant though. Growing up with several failures but he never lost his self-confidence. We hope everyone will love to read his writings.

Instagram Handle: @trapatale

Life is like a hurdle race

Life is like a hurdle race, we have to either surrender or just jump again and again to move forward. It is not so easy to get what you dreamt for, difficult roads often leads to beautiful destination. The day you find out the reason of your life, is the day when you lost afraid of failures. Coward dies several time before his actual death. Extensive success will be ours if we work harder in any situation without losing hope. Challenges are what makes your life interesting and overcoming them makes your life beautiful. We have to take austere decision in hard time. Make your life restless for taking chances otherwise in the end you will regret for the chances you did not take. All of us for certain time we think that we have all time but reality is life gives only one chance, we have to make it worth remembering.

In life, learn to love the sound of your feet walking away from things not meant for you. World is full of fake people don't be too dependent on others. There are things we don't want to know but have to learn, don't want to happen but have to accept it. Be strong now because things will get better. It might be stormy now, but it can't rain forever. This is life buddy good thing takes time. Result is always a reflection of your work. No matter it is our life or in our exam.

There are so many people out there who will always tell you that you can't do it. Just say watch me and enjoy their presence while you are building your own emperor of your life.

Sabbi Ansari

Co-author Sabbi Ansari, she is a good writer from Bhagalpur, Bihar. She has completed her Inter in science stream and currently pursuing B.Sc maths honours. She has been writing poetry from almost half years as her passion. She wants to be a teacher in future.

Instagram Handle: @poet_and_pancakes

दिल की बातें

(1)

"ज़िन्दगी में पछतावा करना छोड़ दीजिए
बल्कि,
कुछ ऐसा कीजिए की लोग आपको छोड़ कर पछताए...!"

(2)

खुद को गले लगाना सीख लो,
ताकि बाद मे
तकिये को गले लगाके रोना न पड़े!!

(3)

अकेले जीना सीख लीजिए जनाब,
ये दुनिया बड़ी मतलबी हैं,
दिल लगवाकर, अक्सर दिल से
निकल दिया करती हैं!

(4)

कमाल है ना बिखरे सब अंदर से है यहां,
पर सवार सिर्फ जिस्म को रहे है!

(5)

चलो मुस्कुराने की वजह ढूंढते हैं...
ऐ जिन्दगी तुम हमें ढूंढो...हम तुम्हे ढूंढते हैं
सौदा मंजूर है ना?

(6)

अपना कीमती वक्त उन्ही को केवल दे,
जिनकी नज़र में आप कीमती हो!

(7)

इस करोना काल मे दिन भर मे इतनी
दफा हाथ साफ करते हो,
कभी दिल भी साफ कर लिया होता तो
कितना अच्छा होता!

Kavita Bhatt

Kavita Bhatt, an IT consultant by profession and a poet at heart! Hails from Uttarakhand, author of "Mannmugdha-Ek Soch", "Sacche Pankh" and "Pocket of Smile" found nature as her primary source of poetic inspiration. She likes to read ancient history, love to develop and create mobile applications.
Also Contributed as co-author in "Shades of Pain in her Eyes", "Tinkles of Rhymes", "The Secret Temptation", "Ashes of Maroon", "Girls paradise-2", "Still something is missing-3", "For you mother", "The Lost Puzzle", "Wait Till I Tell You", "Kuch ankahe se alfaaz", "Soo much in Love" and "Jar of Half Wishes".
She can be reached at:
E-mail id: kavitabhatt1506@gmail.com

Instagram Handle: @mannmugdha15

That Benign Journey

The unborn bound which began so slow
Long veiled wades through my silences.
Be holding the melody attuning my success
A sight clear, steering my pave amidst that chaos.

It takes a soul to root the dreams
Claim it with struggle, some says it is so brute.
Scribble your tiny steps every day to surmount it.
An occult presence stares it's all the boundaries.

The mere substance lies within, roar so high.
Chaste the vivid sky so high and submerged to ocean so deep.
The barren earth holding my roots turns so fertile.
Budding new hopes and twilight welcomes my life with pride.

Sharvari Sangam Patil

She don't want to be someone that society wants her to be. She is okay with not being perfect cause that's perfect to her. She believe everyone is on earth for a purpose. She is grateful that she found her purpose. It is to write and help others to find their purpose.

Instagram Handle: @ohh_mere_khudayaa

You are enough

People tell you "you can't pass the test"
You can't be the best
Success is not your cup of tea
But they have the haven's key
All of this statements are bluff
Let me tell you "you are enough".

They things you are not worth it
All they want is you to quit
They are expert in pulling you down
Because they don't want you to achieve crown
Fighting against them will be tough
Let me tell you "you are enough".

You are everything and more
You can be someone that world never have seen before
They won't believe in your truth
But I know and so do you that you can lead the youth
Don't get capture in societies expectations cuff
Let me tell you "you are enough".

You can be anything you want
A lawyer, a doctor, an artist
Swimmer, a pilot, a physicist
Don't be someone that they insist
Your path might be rough
Let me tell you "you are enough".

Pratham Mittal

He is very Positive, kind, helpful, friendly and happy soul. His passion is painting and writing. He has won many competitions, He has been Co-authored of 55+ Anthology and has compiled 5+ Books in which one had recognized by OMG Books of Record & Bravo International Book of World Records - Speaking My Truth, participated in International Writing Competitions.

Instagram Handle: @_pratham2426

Have You Earned Your Tomorrow

Is anybody happier because you passed his way?
Does anyone remember that you simply spoke to him today?
This day is nearly over, and its toiling time is through;
Did you provides a cheerful greeting to the friend who came along?
Or a churlish kind of "Howdy" then vanish within the throng?
Were you selfish pure and straightforward as you rushed along the way,
Or is someone mighty grateful for a deed you probably did today?
that you simply simply helped one brother of the various that you passed?
Is a single heart rejoicing over what you probably did or said;
Does a person whose hopes were fading now with courage look ahead?
Did you waste the day, or break down, was it well or sorely spent?
Did you allow a trail of kindness or a scar of discontent?
As you shut your eyes in slumber does one think that God would say,
you've got earned another tomorrow by the work you probably did today?

Jayashree Sahoo

Jayashree Sahoo is habitant of ODISHA.
She is Co-author of 200+ anthologies. Also she is Compiler of many anthologies in Hindi, English and Odia languages.
According to her, if you don't express your inner feelings towards someone, then just write those on a paper and making yourself happy for without reason.
Among of these extra activities She studying Nursing on govt medical and she has an aim for be a RN nurse and good writer.
Email.id- jayashreesahoo665@gmail.com

Instagram Handle: @mixing_of_emotions

Self motivation

World is so peculiar,
And we man are so jealousy with each other,
I know, I'm the best and unique on my way,
But there some people who don't want my goodness,
There a lot of people who are saying too many words in my back,
They discourage me for doing something,
They always show me that
I'm wrong,
I'm doing mistake,
It's too much bad which I'm doing,
What's the hell where I listen those,
But I never go back again,
I give my best in front of theirs,
I show them that,
I'm not worst
I'm best in my way,
I achieve my success by my hardwork,
Not to listen those words.
So shouldn't listen people,
We should create our own creation by own hardwork and strong confidence,
That I'm sure do that best and all will be well!!

Ipsita Panigrahi

A carefree, joyful, realistic in practical life but she enjoys to live in an imaginative and fictional world. This is Ipsita Panigrahi, a budding writer, who loves to express her feelings and emotions through writings. She hails from Bhubaneswar -the city of temples, Odisha. She has a passion for literature, as she loves to do all those stuff which makes her happy and literature is one among them. She is likely to be called as a scribbler. She finds peace in gardening and reading books and an artist is also hidden in her.

Instagram Handle: @_ipsi_19

Wounded...but still living...!

Blood pours out when I was stabbed,
Not by the strangers but by the most trusted rangers.
It shed, not from my body but from my soul.
I was fired from outside but the inside I roared.

Blood dropped from my eyes,
instead of tears.
I seem so strong but deep ingrained I was shattered by my fears.
No rainbows, no sunshine can make me hear my voice.
Only I can find, the rain and storms making the noise.
I am now the wounded lioness,
Who could found to be senseless.
But still have some blood in her nerves,
And surviving for the day of betrayal to
witness.

Archishman Satpathy

Archishman Satpathy, often called the Enthusiast Writer is a young dynamic writer from Deogarh, Odisha. He is presently pursuing B.Tech from IIIT Bhubaneswar. He started writing Quotes and Short Poetries from a young age of 16 and had now made it as his passion. He has contributed as co-author in more than 80 anthologies. He is the author of the book "LAKEEREIN ZINDAGI KE". Though he has a passion of writing quotes in any instance, he has also a deep love for Cricket.

EITHER WIN OR LEARN

Hey lovely unsuccessful dude standing
What are you watching and thinking?
Are you still in the thought of failure
Or else wants to remember the moment
How you lost and then faces criticism
Am I correct buddy, or something else
Believe me I have a great idea for you
From where you left, start thinking from there
Just idealising the process or proceedings
May God give you a chance to think about
You have to try again and that too now
From where you left, start trying from there
Definitely you will learn something more
And may succeed in this attempt dude.

WILL TRY TILL DOOM

Never ever I thought of the criticism
Just believes the fact everytime that
Either you will win or learn something
Tried to give off but thanks conscience
Shall I try once again is my question and
Everytime I get the answer of "YES"
Just because I was close to win last time
I can never thought of giving off also
Trying to synchronise my soul into fate
Now I am going to try my luck with sound
Whatever the result will be, can't break me
If possible I will try till the doom and gloom
Lets fly in the high sky of life happily ever
And achieve the horizon into our pockets.

Aman Sharma

Aman Sharma is currently pursuing his Bachelor's in Maths Honours but he is most interested in expressing his thoughts through his writings. Having a very intellectual mind which has a deep desire to explore the truth and causes of life and it's dilemma. He is also a co-author in about 15 anthologies. Let's see what he have for you today.

Instagram Handle : @aman_shaan

I need a change!

I feel nothing!
I don't know why,
But I feel less,
Surely there's something
May be I have felt too much,
That I started to feel nothing.
Nothing seems new,
Nothing appears exciting.
May be this just happens with age,
Or may be I am just too bored,
everything feels less, everything feels void.
Morning breeze is chilling no more,
Rain doesn't wet me anymore,
Vision appears colourless,
Sunset not so illuminating any more.
Festivals now only means a holiday.
Outings are not so exciting.
______ doesn't effect me much.
What is it, does that happens with everyone or is it just me!?
Where's all that excitement gone?
Life has become monotonous and everything is blown!
What I need is a CHANGE!

Vivek Santosh

Dr. VIVEK SANTOSH (pursuing MBBS). Medico by profession with a artist inside. Love to do Poem Writing, Painting, Wildlife Photography and Guitarist.

अपने इस व्यस्त जिंदगी से जब भी कुछ पल चुराता हूँ,
आप सबो के लिए कुछ प्यारे अल्फ़ाज़ लिख जाता हूँ।

Contact- viveksantosh11@gmail.com

Instagram Handle: @vivek_santosh

कामयाबी के साथ रिश्ता

ये डगर बहुत कठिन है प्यारे,
इसकी ये राहे अनजान सही।
कामयाबी को तू काम मत आँक,
इस से रिश्ता जोरना इतना भी आसान नही।

पर कहाँ लिखा है कि असंभव ना संभव हो पाया है,
जीता वही है जो हमेशा तूफान से टकराया है।

जिस दिन ये हुनर तू सीख गया प्यारे,
तेरे सामने कामयाबी भी शीश झुकायेगी।
चाहे उस दिन अपने साथ दे ना दे,
पर उस पल कामयाबी साथ निभाएगी।

इसलिए कभी निराश ना हो,
कर वही जो तेरे मन में हो।
एक दिन नाकामयाबी भी तुम्हारे सामने झुकेगी,
और फिर जग में तुम्हारी जयकार गूंजेगी।

कामयाबी और मनुष्य का रिश्ता ही बड़ा अनोखा है,
जिसने भी दिल से निभाया उसे मिला ना धोखा है।
जिसने भी इसे एक तपस्या मानी,
उसने सब कर दिखाया जो भी उसने ठानी।

तुम भी आज ठान कर आगे बढ़ जाओ,
और असंभव को संभव कर दिखाओ।
उस दिन पूर्ण हो जाएगी मन की हर आशा,
तभी तो सार्थक होगी कामयाबी के साथ रिश्ते की परिभाषा।

Flairs and Glairs, a platform by a student for the students. We are esteemed youth struggling to carve out our path for our future and we follow a basic mindset Since everyone is not born with all-round skills. Joining hands with people who are born to execute it with perfection is the best way to evolve. Self-Evolution is the need of the hour but, evolving as a community is what we strive for. The initiative as kickstarted by, Founder- Mr. Shubham Shah with the motive to utilize the skillset and talent of writing has now a team of 10+ people who are actively participating into newer forms of learning and discovering talents among youngsters. We Provide platform and services like Publishing opportunities, Open mics, Workshops, Hands-on training. Operating with Brand Name of Flairs and Glairs (Publication House), we offer the chance of elevating a passionate writer to an esteemed author With Brand name Teekhe Zasbaaat. We bring to you an opportunity to get accustomed with the Public Speaking and Presenting of Thoughts along with regular challenges to brush up your inking spirit. The newest initiative to extend our services we introduced in a new writing Platform- The Glittering Fables and Ink Over Tears.

We Choose to Fly Like A Falcon than to

be a Leg Pulling Crab.

To Know More: Infoline – 7781900870
Mail Us At-
flairsandglairs@gmail.com / info@flairsandglairs.in
Or Visit is at
www.flairsandglairs.com / www.flairsandglairs.in
Social Handles- @flairsandglairs @teekhezasbaaat

www.ingramcontent.com/pod-product-compliance
Ingram Content Group UK Ltd.
Pitfield, Milton Keynes, MK11 3LW, UK
UKHW022005190726
13853UKWH00004B/1738